A VISIT TO
AUSTRALIA

Story by Mary Packard
Illustrated by Benrei Huang

A GOLDEN BOOK • NEW YORK

Western Publishing Company, Inc., Racine, Wisconsin 53404

D1495941

Ted Fletcher is nine and lives in the town of Manly, Australia, or *down under* as the *Aussies* like to say. Ted wants to be a champion surfer when he grows up. Since he can walk to the beach from his house, he gets to practice a lot.

Another great thing about Manly is that it's just a short ferry ride to Sydney, Australia's largest city. Ted's father owns a jewelry store there, and his mother is head zookeeper at the Taronga Park Zoo.

It was the week after Easter, the "Autumn Holiday," when schools and many businesses were closed. Ted's father had flown to the opal fields at Coober Pedy, in hopes of finding some of the fiery gems to sell in his store.

Mrs. Fletcher had a few days off, so she and Ted decided to go camping in the Blue Mountains, a few hours' drive west of Sydney. They set up camp and decided to try to catch their lunch.

"There's a platypus!" cried Ted as he and his mother fished in the stream near their campsite. Ted aimed his camera at the strange-looking creature and snapped its picture.

Ted and his mother ate the trout they caught and then took a walk. They hadn't gone far when Mrs. Fletcher pointed to a eucalyptus tree and whispered, "Look, Ted." There, sitting still as a statue on a very high branch, was a mother koala with her baby clinging firmly to her back.

Suddenly a mother kangaroo and her baby came quite close to them. "There's a *joey*!" Ted cried, snapping a picture of the *roo* and her baby.

That night, as Ted and his mother were about to get ready for bed, they heard a pitiful cry and went to investigate.

"It's a baby wombat," said Mrs. Fletcher. "Something must have happened to its mother. Don't worry," she crooned to the forlorn little creature. "We'll take good care of you back at the zoo."

Back home a few days later, Ted's mother reminded him about the baby wombat.

"Since it's Easter break, we're a little shorthanded at the zoo," she said. "I wondered if you would like to take care of the baby wombat at home. It still needs to be fed every few hours, and I will pay you to do it."

"I'd love to!" cried Ted. "Then I can get that surfboard I've been saving for even sooner!"

Mrs. Fletcher brought the baby wombat home that night. When it was feeding time, she handed the wombat to Ted, along with a baby bottle.

"I think I'll call him Willy," said Ted as he sank down into a chair to feed him.

The next day, Ted's grandmother came to stay with him while his mother was at work. Ted set his alarm clock to remind himself when to feed Willy. By the end of the day, the little wombat was greeting him with happy squeaks.

The following morning, Grandma had planned to go to the dentist in Sydney.

"Aren't you coming with me?" she asked Ted. "We'll have a picnic lunch afterward."

"I'd love to," Ted replied, "but I can't leave Willy alone."

"Of course you can't," Grandma said. "Your mum said we could take him along in a basket," she added.

Ted put Willy in a basket, and packed several baby bottles in his knapsack. Then they set out on the ferry for Sydney.

"Don't be afraid, Willy," said Ted. "We'll be back on land before you know it."

But Willy wasn't frightened at all. In fact, the motion of the boat had rocked the baby to sleep.

As they approached the shore, Willy poked his head out of the basket to look around. Ted pointed to a fantastic-looking building.

"That's the Opera House," he said. "Some Sydney-siders call it 'Operasaurus.' I think it looks like a lot of fishes swallowing each other."

Ted gave Willy a bottle while he waited for Grandma in the dentist's office. When she was finished, they took the bus to Darling Harbor to have their picnic lunch.

"We're in luck," said Ted. "There's a concert in the amphitheater today."

Ted and Grandma settled themselves on the grass to eat their lunch and enjoy the music. They didn't even notice when Willy climbed out of the basket.

Ted finished his sandwich and reached into his knapsack to get a bottle for Willy.

"*Tucker-time, mate,*" he said as he knelt by the basket. But it was empty.

"Oh, no!" cried Ted. "He's gone, Grandma!"

Suddenly there was a scream.

"What's that?" cried Ted.

"I bet I know," said Grandma. "Let's go see."

The screams led to a frightened lady pointing frantically to her picnic basket. Inside it was Willy, snoring contentedly.

"Silly Willy!" Ted said with a laugh. "You've got the **wrong** basket!"

In bed that night, Ted could not fall asleep. Next week he had to go back to school, and the thought of giving Willy up made him sad.

Ted got up and wandered into the kitchen.

"I can't sleep," he announced to his mother. "Willy won't like it at the zoo. Who will comfort him when he's scared? Who will play with him when he's bored?"

Mrs. Fletcher made Ted a glass of nice warm milk.

"Willy will have plenty of other animals to keep him company at the zoo," she said. "Don't worry. We'll take good care of him."

The next morning, Ted went outside to feed Willy before leaving for school. Mrs. Fletcher followed him.

"I've been thinking," she began. "I'm proud of the fine way you've taken care of Willy. Would you like to become a zookeeper's assistant in the Children's Zoo next summer? You could work in the mornings and still have enough time for your surfing."

"Wow!" cried Ted. "Then I could see Willy every day!"

The months flew by and before Ted knew it, summer vacation had begun. Ted's first day as a zookeeper's assistant began with a very big surprise.

"Hey, Willy!" said Ted. "You sure have grown!"

As soon as the little wombat heard Ted's voice, it scurried over to greet him with happy squeaks.

"The name's not Willy anymore," said a zookeeper. "From now on, her name is Wilhelmina. If you look closely at her belly, you can see a pouch starting to form. That's where a mother wombat carries her babies," he explained.

"That's amazing!" exclaimed Ted.

One day, as Ted was getting ready to leave, he stopped to say good-bye to Wilhelmina.

"This is the best summer ever," he told her happily. "And I owe it all to you!"

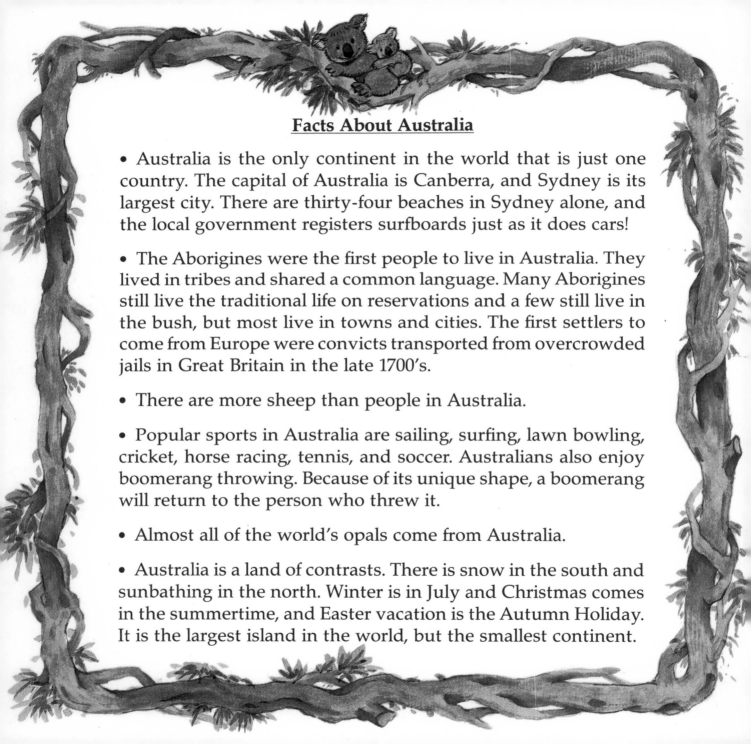

Facts About Australia

• Australia is the only continent in the world that is just one country. The capital of Australia is Canberra, and Sydney is its largest city. There are thirty-four beaches in Sydney alone, and the local government registers surfboards just as it does cars!

• The Aborigines were the first people to live in Australia. They lived in tribes and shared a common language. Many Aborigines still live the traditional life on reservations and a few still live in the bush, but most live in towns and cities. The first settlers to come from Europe were convicts transported from overcrowded jails in Great Britain in the late 1700's.

• There are more sheep than people in Australia.

• Popular sports in Australia are sailing, surfing, lawn bowling, cricket, horse racing, tennis, and soccer. Australians also enjoy boomerang throwing. Because of its unique shape, a boomerang will return to the person who threw it.

• Almost all of the world's opals come from Australia.

• Australia is a land of contrasts. There is snow in the south and sunbathing in the north. Winter is in July and Christmas comes in the summertime, and Easter vacation is the Autumn Holiday. It is the largest island in the world, but the smallest continent.